For Esther and Trini, with love and kisses —S. P.-H.

For Eunice, with love and thanks —S. M.

Text copyright © 2016 by Smriti Prasadam-Halls
Illustrations copyright © 2016 by Sarah Massini

First published in Great Britain in January 2016 by Bloomsbury Publishing Plc
Published in the United States of America in October 2016
by Bloomsbury Children's Books
www.bloomsbury.com

Bloomsbury is a registered trademark of Bloomsbury Publishing Plc

For information about permission to reproduce selections from this book, write to
Permissions, Bloomsbury Children's Books, 1385 Broadway, New York, New York 10018
Bloomsbury books may be purchased for business or promotional use. For information on bulk purchases
please contact Macmillan Corporate and Premium Sales Department at specialmarkets@macmillan.com

Library of Congress Cataloging-in-Publication Data
available upon request
ISBN 978-1-68119-149-2 (hardcover)

Art created digitally using mixed media and collage · Typeset in Filosofia · Book design by Kristina Coates

Printed in China by Leo Paper Products, Heshan, Guangdong
2 4 6 8 10 9 7 5 3 1

All papers used by Bloomsbury Publishing, Inc., are natural, recyclable products
made from wood grown in well-managed forests. The manufacturing processes
conform to the environmental regulations of the country of origin.

Kiss It Better

Smriti Prasadam-Halls

illustrated by
Sarah Massini

BLOOMSBURY
NEW YORK   LONDON   OXFORD   NEW DELHI   SYDNEY

Sometimes you feel a bit down in the dumps.
You've scraped your knee,
you've got bruises and bumps.

Don't worry, a kiss isn't far away . . .

. . . It flies in to find you and saves the day.

A **kiss** for a forehead,

a **kiss** for a nose,

a **kiss** for an elbow,

or **ten wriggly toes**.

It pours out its magic
in each tiny touch,
and tells you each time . . .

"I love you so much."

For did you know **kisses** can actually speak?
Listen the next time one lands on your cheek.

An I'm-sorry kiss helps make amends.

It whispers softly,

"Can we be friends?"

A cheer-up kiss says,
"Tell me what's wrong."

A be-brave kiss
says,
"Come on,
stay strong!"

A see-you-soon kiss
says,

"I'll miss
you, too."

And . . .

. . . a go-to-sleep kiss shouts out,

If thunderstorms wake you up with a fright,
a **sweet-dreams kiss** keeps you safe through the night.

And if you are at home feeling sick,
grab hold of a **get-well-soon kiss**—double quick!

Bad moods or accidents,
all first-time fears,
grumbles and grouches,
tantrums or tears—

it doesn't matter HOW
funny you feel . . .

. . . an
I'm-there-for-you
kiss
soon helps
you heal.

Sometimes, it's strange, just one kiss will do.
Other times, you'll find you need quite a few.

But no matter what your **kisses** are for,
they never run out—there'll always be more!

That's how it works if
you're big and you're tall.

That's how it works
if you're ever so small.

And you'll never guess what—yes, just like you . . .

. . . sometimes GROWN-UPS need kisses, too!

Every day has its ups and its downs.
Sometimes you giggle, sometimes you frown.

But the thing to remember, the secret is this . . .

...EVERYTHING feels better with the help of a **kiss!**